## Hello, Family Members,

Learning to read is one of the most important accomplishments of early childhood. **Hello Reader!** books are designed to help children become skilled readers who like to read. Beginning readers learn to read by remembering frequently used words like "the," "is," and "and"; by using phonics skills to decode new words; and by interpreting picture and text clues. These books provide both the stories children enjoy and the structure they need to read fluently and independently. Here are suggestions for helping your child *before*, *during*, and *after* reading:

### Before

- Look at the cover and pictures and have your child predict what the story is about.
- Read the story to your child.
- Encourage your child to chime in with familiar words and phrases.
- Echo read with your child by reading a line first and having your child read it after you do.

### During

- Have your child think about a word he or she does not recognize right away. Provide hints such as "Let's see if we know the sounds" and "Have we read other words like this one?"
- Encourage your child to use phonics skills to sound out new words.
- Provide the word for your child when more assistance is needed so that he or she does not struggle and the experience of reading with you is a positive one.
- Encourage your child to have fun by reading with a lot of expression . . . like an actor!

### After

- Have your child keep lists of interesting and favorite words.
- Encourage your child to read the books over and over again. Have him or her read to brothers, sisters, grandparents, and even teddy bears. Repeated readings develop confidence in young readers.
- Talk about the stories. Ask and answer questions. Share ideas about the funniest and most interesting characters and events in the stories.

I do hope that you and your child enjoy this book.

—Francie Alexander
    Reading Specialist,
    Scholastic's Instructional Pu

For My Brother Ted
—T.J.

To Zak
—C.C.

Text copyright © 1998 by Roger D. and Susan T. Johnston,
as Trustees of the Johnston Family Trust.
Illustrations copyright © 1998 by Carolyn Croll.
All rights reserved. Published by Scholastic Inc.
SCHOLASTIC, HELLO READER! and CARTWHEEL BOOKS
and associated logos are trademarks and/or registered
trademarks of Scholastic Inc.

Library of Congress Cataloging-in-Publication Data

Johnston, Tony, 1942-
    Boo!: a ghost story that could be true / Tony Johnston;
illustrated by Carolyn Croll.
        p. cm. — (Hello reader! Level 4)
    Summary: While reading about the ghost of Old Clara Clabber, a farmer hears
spooky noises and lets his imagination get out of hand.
    ISBN 0-590-37998-4
    [1. Ghosts—Fiction.  2. Imagination—Fiction.  3. Fear—Fiction.
4. Farmers—Fiction.]  I. Croll, Carolyn, ill.  II. Title.
III. Series.
PZ7.J6478Bo 1998                                     98-20283
[Fic]—dc21                                               CIP
                                                          AC

12 11 10 9 8 7 6 5 4                          02 03 04

Printed in the U.S.A.   23
First printing, October 1998

# BOO!

## A GHOST STORY
### THAT COULD BE TRUE

## BY TONY JOHNSTON
## ILLUSTRATED BY CAROLYN CROLL

Hello Reader! — Level 4

SCHOLASTIC INC.

Cartwheel
B·O·O·K·S·®

New York   Toronto   London   Auckland   Sydney

It was a dark and scary night on a farm.
It was as dark as the inside of a cow.

A farmer was reading to pass the time.

He was reading about Old Clara
Clabber, who drowned in pickle juice.

On nights like this, her ghost was known to float about and whine.

A wind whipped up.

It began to wail, "Wooooo!"

The farmer stopped reading and listened.

He heard, "Boooo!"
He thought, "That's not wind. It's Clara
Clabber's ghost!"

armer was spooked. So he sang
lf a song. He sang about green
of grass, which cows chew in
3.

But green was the color of pickles. And pickles reminded him of pickle juice. And pickle juice reminded him of...Clara Clabber's ghost!

"Booooo!" The ghost was close.

Its moan squeezed through the knot holes of the house.

What if the ghost squeezed in, too?
What if it squeezed him?

The farmer lugged his laundry out, hankies and socks and such. Then he plugged up every knot hole with clothes.

"The sniff of a hound couldn't slip in now." He hoped.

"Booooo!" moaned the ghost.
It sounded as close as his shadow.
He stood stiff as a scarecrow, waiting
for it to pounce.

But he thought, "No ghost grabs me without a fight!"

Then he felt tough enough to tie the ghost into a knot. So he opened the door.

"Come on, Clara Clabber!" He roared. "Try to clobber me!"

"MOOOOOO!"

"Miss Grass!"

The farmer was so glad to see his cow, he gave her a kiss.

"Come on in," he said.
So she did.

t wasn't dark anymore. The sun was
coming up. The farmer got a stool and
milked Miss Grass.

The farmer wasn't scared anymore.
He drank a glass of milk—and ate
a pickle.

Then he unplugged the knot holes, got dressed, and went outdoors to finish his chores.